THIS BOOK
BELONGS TO

The Adventures of
Bella & Harry
Let's Visit Saint Petersburg!

Written by
Lisa Manzione

Illustrated by
Kristine Lucco

Bella & Harry, LLC

"WOW! Bella, I have never seen anything so beautiful."

"I agree, Harry. This is called the Grand Palace. It is part of the Peterhof Palace complex (which is now a museum) and it is very beautiful. In the early 1700s, the Grand Palace was built by 'Peter the Great.' There are also lovely fountains, gardens, and parks around the Grand Palace."

"Bella, who was Peter the Great?"

6

"He was a 'tsar' of Russia. His name was 'Tsar Peter I,' but he called himself Peter the Great. He was a strong leader and made a lot of changes in Russia when he ruled the country."

"What is a tsar, Bella?"

"Long ago, tsar was a term used for a male ruler or emperor, usually from Russia."

"I know, Harry. You want to be tsar one day."

"Yes, I do, Bella!"

TSAR PETER I

"**Hey,** Bella, what is that body of water just past the fountain?"

"Harry, that body of water is the Gulf of Finland."

"Gulf of Finland? I thought we were in Russia, Bella."

8

"**We** are in Russia. Let's look at our map together so we know exactly where we are now."

Norway

Sweden

Baltic Sea

Finland

Gulf of Finland

● Saint Petersburg

Russia

⭐ Moscow

"**Saint** Petersburg, Russia is here.

The Gulf of Finland is here. The Gulf leads to
a larger body of water called the Baltic Sea.

The country of Finland is north of Russia."

"**Just** for fun, Harry, we are going to travel by boat back to Saint Petersburg. The boat ride should be an exciting way to return to the city and it only takes about thirty minutes."

"Whew! That is a fast boat, Bella."

"Yes, Harry, it is. The boat is called a 'hydrofoil' and it goes very fast. Remember when we went to Crete during our visit to Athens? We rode in a hydrofoil boat there, too."

"Yes, we did!"

"**Look,** Harry, it is the State Hermitage Museum. The State Hermitage Museum's main complex is made up of six buildings: Winter Palace, Small Hermitage, Old Hermitage, New Hermitage, Hermitage Theater, and Reserve House. The main building is the Winter Palace. Beginning around the year 1760, the Winter Palace was the main home of the tsars of Russia. The beauty and grand style of this palace make it one of the most popular museums in Russia (and maybe the world) today."

14

"The three-story Winter Palace is painted a pretty color of green and white and has Baroque architecture (which we learned about when we visited Rome). The palace has 1,786 doors, 1,945 windows, and more than 1,000 rooms and halls."

"Wow, Bella, this is one big house."

"And a very fancy house too, Harry."

15

"Let's explore the museum, Harry."

"Bella, let's race up the staircase!"

16

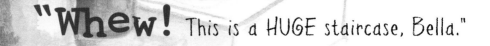

"**Whew!** This is a HUGE staircase, Bella."

"I agree, Harry. The staircase is called the 'Principal,' or 'Jordan,' Staircase of the Winter Palace. This staircase was originally used by the tsar during special events relating to the Neva River."

"Harry, why don't we join the walking tour of the museum now? I don't think I can run anymore!"

"Okay, Bella. Where will the walking tour take us?"

"Well, we definitely want to see the Rembrandt and Matisse paintings that the Hermitage has."

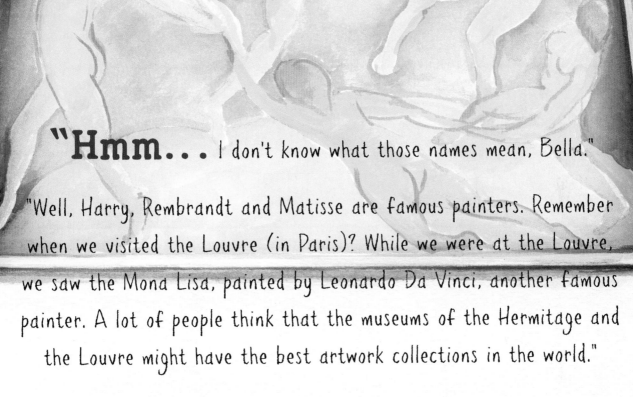

"**Hmm...** I don't know what those names mean, Bella."

"Well, Harry, Rembrandt and Matisse are famous painters. Remember when we visited the Louvre (in Paris)? While we were at the Louvre, we saw the Mona Lisa, painted by Leonardo Da Vinci, another famous painter. A lot of people think that the museums of the Hermitage and the Louvre might have the best artwork collections in the world."

"Oh yeah, I remember. I think my favorite painter in this instance is Matisse. Bella, do you agree?"

"Yes, I do!"

19

"**Bella,** look at this room! It looks like we are in Cairo (located in the country of Egypt) again."

"**Yes,** Harry. This room is called the 'Hall of Ancient Egypt.' One of the main treasures here is the statue of Pharaoh Amenemhat III. This pharaoh ruled thousands of years ago. Learning about world history should be very important to everyone, even if it is not about their own country."

"Ohhhhhhhh..."

21

"**This** is a *HUGE* museum, Bella."

"Yes, it is, Harry. We are going to take a break, have lunch,
and then take a nap. We have a great evening ahead of us.
We are going to the Russian ballet!"

"**Ballet?** Why are we going to a ballet in Russia?"

"The Russian ballet is very famous and a 'must see' when in Russia. It will be magical, I promise."

"Let's sit down and enjoy our lunch now. We are having a typical salad, which we would call potato salad. It has potatoes, carrots, peas, eggs, mayonnaise, pickles, and chicken (or other meat) all mixed together. Our second course is called 'borscht' (a soup made with beets) and it is served with sour cream on top. The last course is called 'kotleta po kievski', also known as Chicken Kiev, which is a fried chicken cutlet filled with a butter made of garlic, onions, and herbs."

"Yummm. That food was great, Bella."

"Nap time."

"**Bella,** our family looks very nice in their fancy outfits."

"Yes, they do, Harry. It is nice to see them dressed up for the ballet."

Just as everyone was getting seated,
Harry noticed Bella was nowhere in sight.

Oh no!, Harry thought. Bella is going to
miss the ballet. Where could she be?

Just as the curtain began to rise, Harry could not believe his eyes. Bella was on stage! Bella was dancing with the ballet dancers!

28

Harry did not know Bella had been chosen to perform the opening of the ballet with the ballet company. When Bella returned to her seat, she was the happiest Chihuahua in the whole wide world.

"Oh, Harry, my dream has come true! I danced with the famous Mariinsky Ballet. I just knew this night would be magical."

"**Harry**, did you know that the Mariinsky Ballet (formerly known as the Imperial Russian Ballet or Kirov Ballet) dates back to the eighteenth century? This ballet company is considered to be one of the greatest ballet companies in our world today."

"WOW! You were very lucky, Bella, and a great ballet dancer too."

"Yes, Harry, I was very lucky. I wish we could dance all night, but we need to head to the train station now."

31

Harry and I had a great time visiting Saint Petersburg with our family. We hope you can join us on our next adventure, but for now it's "do svi danya," or good-bye, in Russian, from Bella Boo and Harry too!

32

Our Adventure to Saint Petersburg

Bella playing with matryoshka dolls, also called Russian nesting dolls.

Bella and Harry visiting the Church of Our Savior on Spilled Blood in Saint Petersburg.

Playing in the Gardens of Catherine Palace (also known as the Great Palace of Tsarskoye Selo) located in Tsarskoye Selo (Pushkin), Russia.

Bella visits the Cathedral of Vasily the Blessed, commonly known as Saint Basil's Cathedral, a former church in Red Square in Moscow, Russia. This building in now a museum.

Fun Russian Words and Phrases

Yes – Da

No – Nyet

Thank you – Spasibo

Hello – Privet

Good-bye – Do svi danya

Good morning – Dobre utro

Good afternoon – Dobre den

Good night – Dobre vecher

Library of Congress Cataloging-in-Publications Data is available

Manzione, Lisa

The Adventures of Bella & Harry: Let's Visit Saint Petersburg!

ISBN: 978-1-937616-53-3

First Edition

Book Thirteen of Bella & Harry Series

For further information please visit:

BellaAndHarry.com

or

Email: BellaAndHarryGo@aol.com

Printed in the United States of America

Phoenix Color, Hagerstown, Maryland

July 2014

14 7 13 PC 1 1

DATE DUE

MAR 07 2016		
APR 04 2016		
APR 26 2016		
MAY 09 2016		
MAY 23 2016		
SEP 26 2016		
OCT 10 2016		
OCT 24 2016		
NOV 14 2016		
DEC 05 2016		
JAN 16 2017		
MAR 14 2017		
APR 03 2017		
		PRINTED IN U.S.A.